# Butterfly Kisses

### by Bob and Brooke Carlisle
### illustrated by Carolyn Ewing

*Inspired by the song written by Bob Carlisle and Randy Thomas*
*© 1996 Diadem Music Publishing & Polygram International Publishing Inc.*

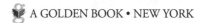 A GOLDEN BOOK • NEW YORK

www.goldenbooks.com
www.randomhouse.com/kids
Educators and librarians, for a variety of teaching tools, visit us at www.randomhouse.com/teachers
Library of Congress Control Number: 97-74418
ISBN: 978-0-307-98872-0
Printed in the United States of America
23 22 21 20 19 18 17 16 15 14 13

*Forever and for always—*
*That's how a Daddy loves his girl.*
*To Mommy and me you'll always be*
*The most beautiful girl in the world.*

And Daddy, I remember when
You first showed me this:
You brushed my cheek
    with your long eyelashes
And said that's how butterflies kiss!

*I* tickled your cheek,
    and I'll tickle your feet,
'Cause I love to hear you giggle.
And I'll hug you here,
    close to my heart,
No matter how much you wiggle!

Toes on toes and dancing around,
We twirl across the floor.
"It's time for bed," you start to say.
And I laugh, "Just one dance more!"

*When I watch you say*
*your prayers at night,*
*I say a little one, too,*
*Thanking God for giving me*
*A precious girl like you.*

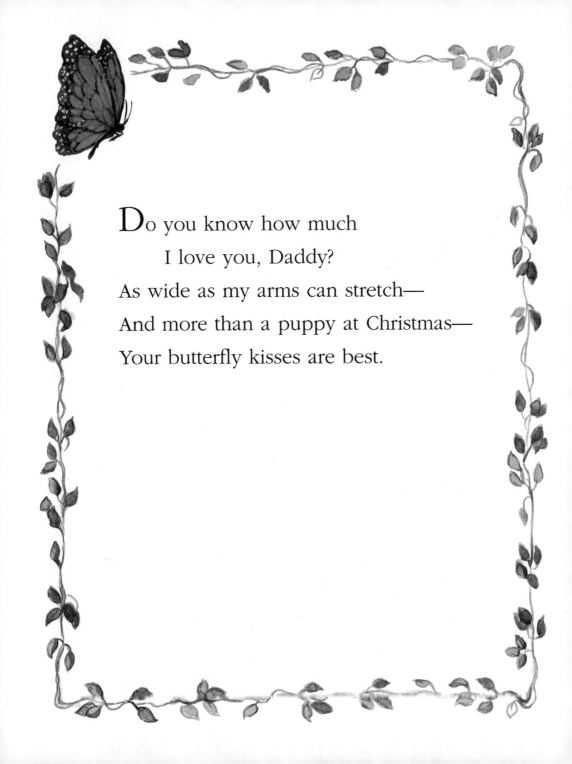

Do you know how much
  I love you, Daddy?
As wide as my arms can stretch—
And more than a puppy at Christmas—
Your butterfly kisses are best.

*The cakes you baked me,*
  *the presents you made,*
*The time you went onstage to sing;*
*I'm always so proud to be your dad—*
*I feel just like a king!*

Your hugs in the morning
  and stories at night,
And fun times in-between;
You make me so glad I'm your
  little girl—
I feel just like a queen!

*The time will come—I know it will—*
*When you're going to fly away*
*In a lovely, flowing, lacy gown*
*On your wedding day.*

You said you'll be there at my side
To walk me down the aisle.
I'll be all dressed up, I'll be a bride,
But it's you who'll make me smile.

And when I'm grown up and married
And have a little girl, too,
I'll show her our butterfly kisses
And love her like I love you.

*I love you, my little girl.*
I love you, too, Daddy.